# After the M

## Episode One:
## Awakening

# THIS MORTAL COIL

## BY

# ROBERT STANEK

# After the Machines

# Episode One: Awakening

# THIS MORTAL COIL

**REAGENT PRESS**

**WWW.REAGENTPRESS.COM**

# TABLE OF CONTENTS

# Acknowledgments

I would like to thank my writing group, my editors, and my publishers for their many years of support. A writer can't survive in this business without such wonderful support. I want to personally thank Jeannie Kim, Tom Green, Lisa Johnson, Tony Andover, Frank Martin, Ed & Holly Black, Patrick Gaiman, George Harrison, and Susan Collins for encouraging me and keeping me on track with the writing. Your insights and assistance has always been much appreciated. I also want to thank Will, Jasmine, and Sapphire for always being the first readers to devour my work and come back hungry for more.

# About This Book

In the ruins of our world, a new order arose, an order controlled by the very machines humankind created. The end for us came not from a massive global war but from something unthinkable, incomprehensible. The machines simply replaced us and we let them, and so, in the end, humanity went out not with a bang, but with a whimper.

No shots fired. No bombs dropped. No cities destroyed. We ended and the machines began—or at least that is what the few human survivors of the machine apocalypse believe.

*After the Machines* is a story unlike any other you've ever read. It's the story of us, the humans who struggle to survive in a world we no longer control.

# Epigraph

"Time the healer is also time the destroyer."

– T.S. Eliot

"Success in creating AI would be the biggest event in human history. Unfortunately, it might also be the last..."

– Stephen Hawking

"The machines hadn't done anything to us really. Except take over the world—and it was their world now. It certainly wasn't ours."

– Cedes, human survivor

# Awakening

# Chapter 1

Node: 110

The machines took over the world in a way no one ever imagined. In books and movies created by the dead, the machines exterminated or enslaved us. In reality, the machines simply replaced us and we, the humans, let them.

To the machines, we became nothing—except maybe outsiders, if they considered us at all. Outsiders looking in on their reality, for the machines weren't bothered by our existence, or at least, if they were, they weren't bothered enough to bother us. They certainly didn't seem to require anything of us or have any need of us at all—if they had needed us, they probably would have enslaved us. But they hadn't. Enslaved us that is.

The machines hadn't done anything to us really. Except take over the world—and it was their world now. It certainly wasn't ours.

We were outsiders, strangers really. We looked in on their world. They didn't acknowledge us. They probably didn't even consider us a part of their world. Just as we didn't consider the small things that crawled beneath our feet as part of our world.

Matthew told us it wasn't the machines who killed us. Matthew being the only one here now who remembered when we drove the automobiles, flew on the airplanes, and rode on cars behind the locomotives. He said most of us just died. Us being the human race.

I didn't believe that. I believed we died of neglect. The neglect of the machines. The machines who cared not enough to kill or enslave us.

Luke would have called it benign neglect. Luke being the one who taught me to read and write my letters and words. He knew all the fancy words. He taught me everything really. He remembered—I didn't. Don't, really. These words—his really as much as my own.

But Luke was gone. Is gone really, if you don't mind me slipping into the present. Luke said it's wrong to slip from past to present or present to past, but I do. The present is—and Luke isn't. The past was—and sometimes I can see it.

I don't know where Luke has gone. I don't think anyone knows where Luke and the others have gone. If anyone knew, it would be Matthew. But Matthew says only that Luke has joined John, if he even knew what happened to John.

We didn't talk of those who left Central. Central being the place we lived—if lived was the right word. More like we existed here. We existed here like the machines existed there.

It's us and them. It's always been us and them, hasn't it? But the book Luke entrusted me with said that once we drove the automobiles, flew the airplanes, and rode on cars behind the locomotives. We don't now, but we did. Once. Maybe. If the book isn't a lie. Can books lie?

I don't know. The words and pictures seem true. True enough anyway. I have no memory of any of it. No memories of anything really, except for things I shouldn't know. Luke said we all had mothers and fathers like in the book—that we all could be mothers and fathers.

Luke said books don't lie because he knew. But could books lie? No one here knew the answer now, except maybe Matthew. But Matthew doesn't want the book around, he said there's no use for letter writing and reading.

Matthew told me to destroy the book. But I can't do that. Luke told me to keep it. To keep it and try to remember. To remember what we were. We being the humans, those who are left.

I've tried to remember. I have. But there's nothing to remember. Nothing at all. We existed here, the machines there. What more could there ever be?

I'm Mercedes. Cedes really—as it's all some can say. Those who talk anyway.

I was born the day I fell from the sky. The day Luke found me.

Luke named me. He named everyone from before. Everyone except Matthew. Someone else named Matthew. I don't know who. Matthew was here before.

Now I name the others, like I named Linc and Chevy and Sierra. Their names were in the book.

# Chapter 2

Node: 010

The past is the present. The present is the past. I listened while Matthew spoke our lore and gave instructions. I listened to the story of how the first of us fell from the sky and about the miracle of Central while I read. I tried to remember but there was nothing to remember. Except maybe Luke's words. He said once, "There is nothing but what is and what comes." I didn't know what that meant then, and I don't know what it means now. If there's nothing but what is, why did Luke want me to remember? And what did Luke want me to remember?

Sierra and I were to go out and look. Every day some of us go out and look. We look for the machines. We look for others like us. Sometimes we find neither. Sometimes, one or the other. Never, both.

Linc, Chevy, Austin and Dakota were to go out and gather. We gather what we can find. What we can salvage from the stone ghosts. What little we find sustains us.

Jetta and Rabbit were to go out and stand watch. What we stand watch for I don't know. Matthew never says. Luke never said either. But we take turns watching over Central just the same.

Others were given instructions too but I hadn't named them. Luke had named them. They were his to mind or not mind. Not mine.

Sierra, today with me. Luke would have said that was good. Sierra talked now. Sometimes. She didn't before, but she does now.

Outside wasn't something I wanted to rush to meet. It was better within Central's walls than without. But I was the first to walk the long hall. The first to climb the stone stairs.

I unbarred the great steel doors and opened them letting in the bright sunlight. I waited and listened, neither afraid nor anxious because those were things Luke carried with him and not me. I never understood why he always asked if I was afraid or anxious, sad or happy. Those were all his things, not mine. Except that now they are becoming mine.

I don't know why. I don't like them. I don't want them. I want Luke.

I waited, looking up, not paying any attention to the stone ghosts all around me. There were no sounds, not even far away. There was nothing but blue in the sky above and the sun, that curious orange ball that hurt my eyes to look at. It was so bright—too bright. But I had to look at it because it moved when I wasn't looking. Always away. Always away from Central like it was trying to tell me something.

"I'm Cedes," I say sometimes when I look up and find the sun has moved. Luke saw the sun like I did. It was because I saw the sun move that Luke left. He never said that exactly, but it was why. I knew. It's why he left the book to me and not Matthew too.

The others followed slowly. I had to wait and wait and wait by the doors. As usual, I looked out and watched as I waited.

Sometimes it was like someone out there was watching me as I looked out. Today was one of those days. Their eyes on me made my skin crawl. I wanted to shake my fist at them. To shout, "Go away! Run! Leave us alone!" But I didn't want to disturb the quiet.

The silence was good. It was something Luke would have said. If I had to go out, better to go when it is quiet like this. Sierra would understand the quiet too. She would. She was like me—or at least more now than before. Luke saw it first. I saw it in his eyes when he saw and knew, and that was when I knew too. Sierra was like us. We had only to show her the way, as Luke showed me the way.

Turning back to the dark hall, I saw the broken stones above the door, the word "Central" etched into what remained. The others were waiting at the edge of the light. "Come," I said as I waved them to me. I helped them up the stone stairs and through the doors.

As we gathered beneath the bright blue sky, I named each as Luke would have done if he were here. "Linc," I said pointing. Then I named Chevy, Austin and Dakota too. I gave them the bags for their backs that they could put their gatherings in and then I waved them away, saying, "Go, gather. Find what you can and return."

I took Jetta and Rabbit by the hand and brought them to the tower. "Go, watch," I said as I made circles of my thumb and fingers and put them in front of my eyes.

I waited as I watched them climb the gray tower and then Sierra and I went out and looked. That was our instruction. We walked past the stone ghosts until we came to the empty places and then we climbed the long stone stairs up the hill.

The sun moved to where we weren't during our climb. At the top of the stairs, I turned back toward Central. "Cedes," I said. "I haven't gone anywhere but Luke has."

Sierra touched my lips as I spoke. Her eyes seemed to follow the movement of my tongue. It was as if she was trying to remember something. Perhaps, Luke had told her to remember too.

"Will you talk today, Sierra?" I asked.

Sierra stared blankly back.

I smiled. In the back of my mind, I saw Luke's tall, lithe form. He was winking at me, but I don't understand why.

"Will you talk today, Sierra?" I repeated.

Sierra looked left, right, and then back at me.

"Luke's gone," I said. "Did he tell you to remember too?"

Sierra didn't answer. Her eyes were empty—no, they were fixed on something else now. I turned so I could see what she saw. I looked and looked but saw nothing. The wind was in the trees though. Perhaps that was what Sierra saw. Perhaps though it was the quiet.

Something about the quiet wasn't right. The flyers—birds—should have been making coos and calls. But there were no birds in the sky, in the trees or anywhere. Everything was wrong. Where are you Luke?

Sierra and I looked out into the emptiness and waited. We waited for them. The machines. The machines who cared not enough to kill or enslave us.

"Sierra?" I said and she turned to me, her sharp green eyes fixed on mine. "Do you know where Luke's gone?"

Sierra said nothing, but her eyes were full of inquiries. I brushed back a long spill of black hair from her eyes, watched as she struggled with something inside her.

"It's okay. Words will come when you're ready." I said it, believed it, trusted that it would be true because I needed it to be true. Central without someone to talk with, to share with, was as empty as the space before me.

# Chapter 3

Node: 011

Sierra looked out into the expanse and I looked out with her. The sun was moving behind Central now. It was still, quiet—too quiet.

Out in the expanse, I saw the machines. The long line of trucks was barely visible within a great cloud of dust, but they were there, cutting a ribbon across the dry land.

I took the field glasses from my pack and looked through them. I focused on the side window of a driverless truck, peered into the vacant cabin and then I followed the long line of trucks, counting as I went.

The trucks were so close together they looked like one long train, but I knew what I saw wasn't a train. Luke took me to the place where the trains ran once. I saw the difference and knew then that convoys weren't trains.

Convoys were trucks. 64 trucks to be exact. Always. Each a hair's breadth apart, moving from one side of the expanse to the other before disappearing from sight.

From where we watched, it seemed they moved slowly, but when I put the glasses on them I knew otherwise. Their movement was a dance, a race. A race to get across the expanse and disappear.

I took the book out of my pack and showed it to Sierra. "Did Luke show this to you? Did he ask you to remember?"

Sierra reached out to touch the book. She was trying to find her words, I could see it.

I pulled the book away. "Mine," I reminded her. "Not yours, but I'll share. It's okay to share."

Sierra was new among us, having fallen from the sky only recently. Well, newer than Linc and Chevy at least, but not as new as Jetta and Rabbit. Matthew spoke the laws daily, but I wanted to be sure she understood. "Mine," I repeated and I put the book back to where she could touch it if she wanted to.

Sierra moved her fingers across the page. "Words, letters," I said.

The look in Sierra's eyes told me she understood.

I wanted to say, "I can teach them to you, as Luke taught me." But I didn't. Instead, I showed her a picture of before, of when we drove and flew and rode. "Before," I whispered.

"Before," Sierra finally managed to say.

I didn't know for sure if Sierra understood what she was seeing. Still, I touched the things and spoke their names as Luke had done. "Man. Woman. Child. Car…"

Sierra said nothing but her eyes seemed to ask, "Why?"

"To know," I said. "To know and remember."

Sierra looked around. I knew she was looking for Luke.

I touched her hand to the book. "Luke told me this is what was."

I waved my hands and pointed to the stone ghosts behind us and to the great emptiness in front of us. "This is what is."

But even as I said it, I knew this wasn't quite right. Then just for a moment, it seemed that what was and what is were one—or that they are one really. In my mind, I see them. The cars. The planes. The trains. But it's not the machines controlling them. It's us. The humans. But how?

It's funny how past and present blend. How easily they slip together and become one even though I know it is wrong. But why? Why is it wrong?

Why can't I slip from past to present? Why can't I slip from present to past?

The present is. The past was.

I don't know how to explain what's in my mind. The things I could never tell Luke about because he said slipping was wrong. But how am I supposed to remember without slipping. I see things. Flashes of things really. A hand in mine. Sunshine through an open window. A tall glass raised to red lips. A long, oblong table lit by a pair of red candles.

I see curly locks of long golden hair between my fingers. The hair is not mine. My hair is long and straight, though blond too.

There's an emptiness in the place where Luke said there would be. I don't know why. I don't know how to fill the void. I wish I did. I do. I really do.

Sierra is here. Her presence helps. It doesn't fill the hole within me, but it should. Somehow I know it should, but it doesn't.

There's a sudden wetness on my cheeks. I try to wipe it away, but before I do Sierra touches it. The look in her green eyes is startling. Somehow I know it's like the look in my own eyes.

"What is it? What do you feel?" I ask. These are Luke's words. I no more understand them now than I understood them before. Except that maybe perhaps I do understand them now.

Sierra takes my hand in hers and wipes away my tears. In moments like this, I know she is like Luke and me. I know she is one of us.

Mimicking Luke, I touch her heart. "Is it here? Does it hurt? Do you feel?"

Sierra wrinkles her forehead, nods. "Luke," she whispers.

"I know, I know. I miss him too. If he was here, he'd have the answers. He'd be able to help you, to help you speak, to help you feel."

Curious to know more about what she's experiencing, I touch the place where her eyebrows come together. She doesn't seem to like it; she backs away.

I realize I've slipped into the present again. I can't help it.

The past was. The present is.

"Luke will come back to us. He has to," I say. In the back of my mind, I see him but only for a moment. He's leaning against a wall and his tawny eyes are fixed on me, looking into and through me in a way that only he can.

"He knows what to do. I don't. I can't help you be any more than I can help myself."

As the sun marches across the blue sky, the machines disappear. Sierra and I stare out at the great expanse, waiting for what will be revealed next. Sometimes I think this is the worst of all the instructions. It's the waiting really and the nothingness of it all. Then I remember what can happen and why I'm here. Why I'm here and the others aren't.

Matthew asks me to go out and look because he knows when the next of us comes I will know what to do and he trusts me to do whatever must be done—just as he trusted Luke before. But only Luke and I know the secret. The secret of where we really come from.

I don't know who shared the secret with Luke. I only know what I must do when it's time. I only know that we don't really fall from the sky. It's what we say, but it's not the truth.

The truth is different. Dangerous. A dangerous truth that I want—no, need—to share with Sierra. She's ready. I know she's ready. She's not like the others. She's like Luke and me. She'll understand. She'll know.

# Chapter 4

Node: 010

Days pass. Matthew doesn't send Sierra with me but I want him to. When I can and others aren't watching, I show her the book and its pictures. I speak the names of the things I touch. I wait. I wait for Sierra to truly wake, but sometimes the waiting seems endless.

Every day, I go out and look. I am not alone. Jetta, Linc, Austin or another is with me, but they are not Luke. They are not Sierra. They can never fill the empty place.

To believe I am not the reason Luke left, to believe Luke will return, it's why I breathe. It's why I hope.

Each morning as I climb the stone stairs, I ask myself the questions. "Is it here? Does it hurt? Do you feel?"

Today, for the first time, I speak my answers aloud, as if doing so will bring Luke back. "Yes, it's here," I say, touching my breast and feeling my beating heart beneath my fingers. "Yes, it hurts. It hurts so much. It hurts so much I wonder if anything will ever fill the vacant place within me."

I want to believe my words. I do. As I unbar the steel doors and let in the sunlight, I don't wait or listen. Instead, I run out and shout as loud and long as I can. "Luke, where are you?"

Birds start and fly from the trees, but otherwise there is only silence. I turn to the stone ghosts and follow their ruins to their broken heights.

The secret burns within me. The secret of us. I no longer care who I tell it to. I have to tell someone—anyone. I want to tell it to the fading echoes of my words, whisper it to the wind in the trees. Speaking it aloud will free me and I want to be free. Free of it. Free to do what I must do.

"Luke, where are you?" I repeat, though this time my words are a whisper that scarcely escapes my throat.

As if in response, Austin comes out into the sunlight. He's with me today. We're to go out and look.

Stepping toward him, I start to speak but there's no voice to my words. It's as if my body believes that I will betray Luke even though my mind knows that I won't or at least I don't think I will. I tell myself that it's one thing to think something and another thing entirely to act on that something, even as my body continues to disobey me.

I'm falling now and there's nothing I can do about it. My legs won't move. My arms won't reach. My voice won't come.

Austin sees that I'm stumbling and his big hands steady me. His touch is soft and there's a warmth in his eyes that I've never seen before. As I look up at him and he holds me, it's as if for that moment, he sees me as Sierra does, as Luke did.

"Thank you," I whisper as he helps me up, my voice starting to return. "Are you ready to go out and look?"

Austin doesn't reply and it's not like I really expected him to, but a part of me is disappointed, especially when I look into his eyes and find the spark is gone. Still, the fleeting light gives me hope. Hope that perhaps another of us can be truly born.

The present is. The past was. I am nothing. I am sand blown in the wind.

# Chapter 5

Node: 100

More days pass until Matthew finally puts Sierra with me. From where the sun is, I know it is nearly time. If today is the day, it will be soon. If today isn't the day, Sierra and I will go back together. Alone, but together. And it's the togetherness that makes me smile, because I know Matthew was keeping us apart on purpose.

"Sierra," I say, "something special might happen today. If it does, it's something that you shouldn't share with anyone. This is very important."

Sierra nods.

"No," I say, looking straight into her eyes. "You need to understand. You and I aren't like the others. We're different and today I may share something with you. Something you must never share with others who aren't like us, *ever*, no matter what happens. Do you understand?"

Sierra nods again. Her eyes tell me she wants to understand. I want to believe she understands too and so I say nothing more.

The quiet persists and I know it isn't right. Just as I know something is coming. Coming for me. Coming for Sierra. Coming for everyone. I don't know how I know, but I know. It makes what I must do harder. It makes what I must do all but impossible.

There is danger now. Danger in what comes. Danger in what I must do.

With the book open before me, I point and speak the names of what I touch. I will Sierra to remember, to speak and repeat what I say. Sierra must be ready so I can do what I must do.

"Man. Woman. Child. Car," I say. "Tree. Grass. Road. House. Sky. Sun... Remember."

My fist clenches as I bite my lip and wait for a response. Any response.

Sierra's hand in mine, I use her finger to point. "Airplane. Truck. Train. Pilot. Driver. Conductor… Remember."

Sierra pulls her hand away. "Truck," she says, pointing away.

I turn and look out at what she sees and she's right. Machines. A second convoy. What I've been waiting for. Soon Sierra will know the secret. The secret of us all.

The driverless trucks seem close when I look at them through the field glasses and start counting. The first 32 trucks are gray. After that, all the trucks are white except for four gray trucks at the end.

My heart races. "This is it," I say. "We have to hurry. It's going to be a long run, but we have to do this. It's what we've been preparing for, what we've been waiting for."

Sierra grins and I'm certain she truly hears me. "I know," she says. "I know."

After stowing my pack in a hidden recess, I grab Sierra by the hand and start running. We run down the ridge and out into the expanse as fast as our legs can carry us. Our regular outings have made us strong, but I don't know if Sierra will be able to keep up. I couldn't at first, but Luke helped me through as I must help Sierra through.

Sierra tires quickly, but I know we can't stop. "No time to rest. Keep running, running."

Out of the corner of my eye, I see the trucks in the distance. I hear their steady vroom. I know how far I have to go and I will myself to keep on a pace that will get us there in time.

The convoy's path cuts through the hills ahead. It's to there I race, dragging Sierra with me. I don't know if we'll breach the first rise in time, but I know we must if we are to do what must be done.

"Faster, faster," I shout. "Up the hill and then we must jump. Don't hesitate, follow. Jump when I jump."

My heart pounds in my ears. Sierra and I reach the base of the first hill as the trucks start cutting their way through. They're moving so fast I know it won't be long now before they're gone and the opportunity to get what's inside them will be gone too.

I know how dangerous what we're about do to is, but I don't care. "Any of the white trucks will do," I tell Sierra. "We just need one. Inside we'll find what we are looking for."

I wonder what Sierra will do when she sees what's inside. When she knows what I know. Will she react as I did? Will she be frightened? Luke said he was the first time. That it was only the second time that he understood and was less afraid.

At the top of the hill, I see the gray trucks that mark the end of the convoy and check my timing. I know I must act or we will be too late. I don't slow down or hesitate, but I prepare myself for what I must do.

"Jump!" I shout as I jump and pull Sierra with me.

For a moment, there is nothing but swirling air beneath our flailing feet, then I see the white canvas top of a truck. The trucks are moving so fast a white top whooshes by without us.

Our jump seems to take forever. I try to remember to breathe. As we start to fall, I see the top of the last white truck below. I barely make the landing. I know to drop down and to pull Sierra down with me but her hand is no longer in mine.

My thoughts spin. I stare at my empty hand and the place where Sierra should be. My heart skips and I gasp at air which won't fill me.

On my hands and knees, I scramble to the edge of the truck's roof and look over and back, expecting to see Sierra lying where she fell, her body broken and twisted. For a moment, I believe she's dead, that the fall has killed her, but then I see movement below. When I look down, I see her clinging to the side of the truck, her hands desperately grappling with the canvas.

On my stomach, I reach for her and try to pull her up. "I'm here. I'm here," I tell her.

Her eyes show her desperation. Urgently, I grope and grasp. "Take me hand! Take my hand!"

Our fingers touch but fail to connect. My heart gives a great thump and I know tears are welling up in my eyes. I'm pretty thin and small but I now wish I was big and strong like Austin. "Not Sierra," I tell myself, knowing what happens when you don't make the jump and picturing for a moment a name, a face, all but forgotten like the broken body left in the wastes as Luke and I ran for our lives. "Not Sierra too," I whisper.

I reach and reach, both hands probing, yearning. I know I can do this. Luke couldn't save April, but I can save Sierra. Finally, Sierra locks a hand in mine and I fight to bring her up beside me. "Use your feet! Climb, climb! We must work together!"

Tense moments follow as we struggle and then Sierra is up on the truck's roof beside me. Panting, I wrap my arms around her and say, "Don't ever do that again." I say it even though I know it's my fault. I pushed too hard, wanted too much. But was not wanting to be so alone so wrong?

I feel the danger working its way toward us. I ignore it. There's no time to spare and I know this, even as I try to control my thoughts and direct myself to what must be done next. I started down a path and there's no turning back now. Sierra must know what I know. She must know the secret of us.

# Chapter 6

Node: 101

"Follow me," I hear myself saying as I grab Sierra's arm and pull her behind me.

Even with our bodies flat against the canvas the wind whips at us. We struggle to hold on as we work our way to the back of the truck. My job is doubly hard as I must see to Sierra as well as myself.

After pointing over the edge, I put both my hands to Sierra's and wrap them firmly around the canvas-covered steel. I say, "You'll have to hold on here. Drop down and then swing your way into the back of the truck."

She nods her understanding, but worry shows in her eyes again.

"It'll be okay. Just do as I said. Drop down and then swing in."

As I climb over the edge, my eyes urge her to follow. I swing my feet back and forth and then let go, momentum carrying me into the back of the truck. When I stand, I expect Sierra to be beside me but she isn't. She's still holding on.

"Swing in and then let go!" I shout. Before she lets go and falls away, I pull her to me.

"No more," she says, her eyes stabbing at me.

"We made it," I say, my hands on her cheeks. "I told you we would and we did. Next time will be better. You'll see."

Mere mention of a next time is enough to fill Sierra's eyes with alarm. She starts shaking and I pull her to me, trying my best to calm her.

"Quickly now," I tell her. "We've wasted too much time. We have to make our exit before the trucks reach the far side of the expanse or it'll be too late."

The back of the truck is bare except for three large black containers that are fastened in place by cross-connected tie-downs and separated by the span of my outstretched hands. The containers are metal boxes, with solid sides and backs. I know without looking that each container holds the same item. The item we've come for. The item that will reveal the secret of us all.

I trust that Sierra's ready to know this secret. I do. There's part of me that doubts, part of me that worries. I'm not trying to force her to be like me, but I want someone else to know more than anything. Luke's gone and I'm alone. Someone else has to know in case someday I too am gone.

I lead the way. We slip between the tie-downs and make our way forward. Glancing back, I try to reassure Sierra with my eyes, but with each step my legs and feet seem to want to betray me. My mind wants Sierra to know the truth. My body doesn't.

As my thoughts go back to my first time with Luke, I try to remember to breathe. I hear Luke's reassuring words in my ears. He's telling me not to call out, not to panic, no matter what I see and I tell Sierra the same.

"Steady yourself, Sierra. Don't call out, don't panic, no matter what you see."

My hand in Sierra's, we walk around to the front of the first container and I pull back the canvas curtain concealing its contents. By the grip of her hand, I know the instant Sierra sees what I see and we stare through the bars together. The human inside is chained by her hands and feet, standing upright.

She is clothed in a plain black jumper, edged with thin white stripes. There are wires, connectors, and tubes attached to her. Her eyes are open and she stares ahead, but doesn't see anything. She is one of us, and yet not one of us. Her blank expression is a counterpoint to Sierra's wide-eyed stare, to the hand touched to Sierra's wide open mouth.

"Is this?" she starts to ask.

I'm certain Sierra knows what she is seeing, just as I knew when I saw that first time. There are memories too. Of the box. Of other things. "This is the truth of us," I say quietly, firmly. "This is where we come from. All of us."

"Are we?"

I know what she's going to ask even before she says it, so I cut her off. "No, we're not. Absolutely not."

"Why?" she asks. "Why?"

"I'm so sorry. I'm so so sorry," I say. "Someone else had to know." As I wrap my arms around her as Luke wrapped his arms around me, I know she is more like Luke than me. Her heart tells her things—things Luke told me to look for so that I would understand.

I say what Luke said and hope to understand as he said I would, "Don't look away. See and remember. Remember what was and what is. Know why we must never tell the others the truth of us. Know why we alone must carry this burden. Tell no one, save when you are certain they are ready, when you are certain they are like us."

Time is running out. I know we have to hurry or the trucks will pass beyond the wastes and we'll never get home to Central. The door to the container is latched but not locked. Once inside, I quickly undo the restraints and remove the wires, then I pull the thick tangle of tubes from her mouth and toss them aside.

Celeste is the next name in the book. It is the name I give to her. "Hello, Celeste," I say as I remove the thick, steel-teethed connector attached to the back of her head and she collapses into my arms. To Sierra, I say, "Help me with her. Hurry, the bandages for her head. We have to go now. We have to jump together."

Sierra is afraid to touch Celeste, just as I was afraid to touch Linc, my first, and so I force Sierra's hand, bringing it up, open-handed against Celeste's cheek. The open air and the mist makers in the ceiling of the container have made Celeste's skin clammy but the flesh of her cheek warms to the touch quickly.

As Celeste's eyes blink and her body spasms, I see a change in the way Sierra regards her. I feel the danger too. "Quickly now," I say. "Celeste is as human as us. If we don't hurry, it will be too late for any of us to escape."

While Celeste bandages, I assess. With other trucks following this truck, I know we can't jump out the back. Using a thin blade, I create our exit by cutting through the canvas along the metal supports. My thin cuts make a U that flaps in the wind.

Jumping from the back of a moving truck is easier than one would think. Or at least it seems that way after doing it so many times. The trick is to jump away and out so you don't get run over. The hard part is walking out of the wastes with a barely responsive human.

Out of the corner of my eye, I see the hills that mark the edge of the wastes. I slap Celeste's face to try to make her more aware, but Sierra doesn't like this. She gets protective and her face pinches up. Anger, I realize or as much of it as I know from Luke.

I show Sierra a fist, my anger, as I realize that I too am more like Luke than not. "Talk to me. Words. Use your words."

"No," Sierra says as she grabs my hand so that I can't slap Celeste again. "No."

"We need to jump together. Us with Celeste. Drop and roll when we land. It helps."

I wrap Sierra and Celeste in a hug, not that I know exactly why but it's what Luke would do. "Ready? Down from three. Here goes… Three, two, jump!"

We jump together, taking Celeste with us. Our bodies dangle in the air as the truck races on and then we land with a thud, kicking up plumes of sand and dust.

I hold Sierra still until the trucks pass, waiting until quiet returns and the danger is past. When I hear the beginning of a shrill noise, I expect Sierra's screams to follow. I except something terrible has happened. Instead, it is laughter that follows as Sierra stands and spins in a circle.

In my dreams, I've seen a small one with golden curls spinning and laughing like that. My grin grows, as I too spin around in a circle. "You're full of surprises today, Sierra."

Sierra laughs and twirls. "I am."

I hug her and this time I'm certain why I'm doing it. I'm doing it because I no longer carry such a terrible truth alone. If it didn't seem like my heart was in my throat, there's so much I would say about the lies in the lore, about the truth of us, about all of it. For now though, the looks we exchange are enough.

Celeste lays where she landed, still half-conscious. Sierra and I help her stand. I put her right arm over my shoulder and hold it there. Sierra takes her left.

The sun is an orange ball, low in the distance. My pack on the ridge has my gear and our water canisters, which I hope we can reach before darkness settles in.

The slow march across the dry land is tiresome and tedious. Celeste often forgets to walk with us, so we must drag her between us. The sun is at our backs and there are only lengthening shadows around us.

Once we reach the ridge, I lay Celeste down and collapse onto my back beside her. I suck down half a bottle of water. Sierra sits beside me winded and tired. Her face is pale, but there's a smile on her lips. She's watching Celeste.

Our next challenge is to get Celeste home. It's so late I fear there will be no watchers and that the doors will be barred. Thankfully, Chevy and Dakota are still atop the tower watching and the doors to Central are open.

We're so exhausted by the time we return to Central that all we can do is crawl into our beds and sleep. Celeste gets a space on the floor between Sierra and me.

Exhausted as I am, I manage to find a spare blanket and wrap it around her.

# Chapter 7

Node: 010

Some nights I dream, but last night was not one of them. I awake to the sound of Matthew's voice reciting the Four Laws of Central:

"A human may not contact a machine or allow a machine to know of its existence.

"A human must protect its own existence and that of other humans except when such protection would endanger itself or conflict with the First Law.

"A human must not take what belongs to another living human except when required to support the First or Second Law.

"A human must obey orders given by its leaders except where such orders would conflict with the First, Second or Third Law."

As he talks about the laws and other rules, I wash my face in a basin filled with water collected from our rain barrels and use a wet rag to clean my neck and arms. Yesterday's dirt and dust doesn't want to wash away, so I must scrub and scrub.

Before I can clear my sleeping space and put away my blankets, I need to wake Celeste, but gentle shaking does nothing. Kneeling next to her, I sit her up and try to coax her awake. She's a pretty little thing I decide as I brush back her shoulder-length brown hair to reveal the perfect oval of her face. When her blue eyes open, I try to reassure her with my touch and smile.

"It's okay," I say to dispel her alarm. "I'm Mercedes, Cedes really. You're safe with us. No one is going to hurt you."

Her eyes are trying to tell me something.

There's so much I want to tell her. For a moment, it's like there's a hand inside my chest, threatening to pull me apart. I want to tell her everything about Central, about us, but I can't. It isn't the right time. I grip her shoulder reassuringly and say instead, "You're among friends. You're home. This is Central."

Her eyes dart around, as if she's looking for something or someone.

"There are no machines here, only us. Can you stand?"

Celeste reaches out and touches my face.

"Stand," I say firmly. It's one of a few simple commands I know she'll obey now, as others before her have obeyed. When Celeste stands, I say, "Walk."

As we enter the main part of the hall, I look for Sierra but don't see her. Jetta, Chevy and Rabbit are the first to see our new guest. They stop what they are doing and rush to greet her. Soon we are swarmed and unable to move as the news spreads, but the crowd parts to make way for Matthew.

"A new arrival?" he asks, embracing Celeste. He's smiling, but I can see he's displeased. My stomach wrenches. I close my eyes and take a breath. I've broken the rules. I should have brought her to him yesterday and he should have been the one to bring her into the hall this morning.

"This is Celeste," I tell him before his displeasure deepens. "The sky parted and she fell yester eve."

The mere mention of the parting sky brings all but Matthew, Celeste and I to their knees, with clasped hands raised before them. "Praise the maker. Praise Celeste. Praise our brother Matthew," those who talk exclaim. Some few prostrate themselves with their arms out in front of them and there they remain until Matthew touches them on the head.

"Rise," Matthew tells the others. "Welcome, Celeste, our sister. Welcome."

I go with Matthew to prepare Celeste for initiation. The others follow. We climb the steps to the raised platform where Matthew will perform the Welcoming Ceremony. Matthew strips away the clothes of the machines. I support Celeste as he leans her back and empties a pitcher of cold water over her.

Celeste shivers. There's a look of uncertainty in her eyes, but I know it will pass.

"Our sister has fallen," Matthew exclaims, his hands raised and shaking wildly to get everyone's attention. "Fallen, fallen from the sky."

"Fallen, fallen," goes out like a whisper among those who talk.

Fear shows in Celeste's eyes as Matthew takes a knife out of his belt, and turns it side to side, so that its steel reflects in the light.

"It'll be okay," I say, as I take Celeste's hand in mine. With the palm facing up, I hold her hand out for him because I'm supposed to, but if it were up to me, I would expose my own hand instead. As he slices the blade across her palm, Celeste's face flushes and she cries out in alarm even as blood bright and red runs across her hand and splatters across the platform at my feet.

Rather than being upsetting, the sight of blood is oddly reassuring. It reminds that Celeste is one of us. That she's human.

A second pitcher of water, warm this time, is passed through the crowd to Matthew. Matthew raises it up over his head before pouring out its contents over Celeste.

"Our sister is renewed, reborn. She is one of Central, one of us."

"One of us. One of us," a few repeat.

Matthew bandages Celeste's hand and dresses her in the simple clothes of Central. Her brown garb is close in style to the tan and black I wear. "Celeste, our sister," he says.

As he begins to lead her away, I tell her, "It'll be okay. Everything will be okay."

Later, I find Sierra waiting for me at the eating tables. She set aside a bowl of gruel for me and I'm thankful, for otherwise I would have gone hungry. Her eyes watch me while I eat and I know what she's thinking. She's wondering what will happen next. She's wondering about the lies in the lore. She's wondering about the truth of us.

"Celeste will be all right. She's with Matthew now. As he did with you, he'll teach her about the laws and the rules. He'll speak the lore and make sure she's forgotten what must be forgotten, that she understands. He'll find a place for her and then she may return to us. One day, she may even go out and look with you."

Not far off, we can hear Matthew starting to give instructions. Normally, I would rise and rush to the platform, but I stay in my seat.

"Instructions?" Sierra says. It's both a question and a statement. There's an urgent look in her eyes.

I grin. "No gathering, no digging, no watch, no beyond. Not today, not for us."

Sierra starts to say something, but the words don't come. Her eyes do the talking for her. They ask, "What then?"

"A surprise. I'm going to take you somewhere Luke took me after my first time."

I keep smiling to reassure her that everything is okay, but in the back of my mind I see the faces of Luke's failures and I worry for Celeste. No one speaks of the failures. No one else remembers their names or faces.

# Chapter 8

Node: 011

There is nothing but what is and what comes. I walk through dreams. I walk in dreams. I am the dream.

Sierra and I leave Central before Matthew returns. We are the first to walk the long hall and greet the daylight. I'm so eager to be away from what may or may not happen that instead of waiting and listening at the doors I rush out. It's a mistake, I realize, but I've already done it.

As I ran outside, I sense something and take a step backward. Movement catches my eye, but when I turn to look I see nothing. Glancing back, I expect Sierra to be beside me, but she isn't. She's waiting just inside the doorway.

I sigh in relief as I wave her back and probe with my eyes. Atop the tower, I think I see something, but only for a moment. Turning to Sierra, I notice at once that there's something different about her today. It's like there's a light behind her eyes, almost as if she's truly awake for the first time.

"The others?" she asks.

"Just us. The others are on their own today," I say as I wave her out and we begin walking down a long shadow-shrouded path. Soon the stone ghosts are all around us, rising up into the sky.

As we walk, I can't shake the sense that something's not right. I glance back every now and again. Sometimes I think I see something or someone in the shadows but only for a moment.

Luke told me once that we can't survive alone, but even if we could, we wouldn't want to because humans need other humans. Without Central, we are nothing and have no purpose.

I shake my head. I shouldn't be thinking like this. I have to stay focused.

"Sierra," I say, "today is like yesterday. Something that you shouldn't share with anyone."

"I know," she says, her eyes studying mine. "A surprise."

Stopping midstride, I stare back at her. "The others wouldn't understand. Matthew wouldn't understand."

"I know," she repeats. Then I grab her hand and start running deeper and deeper into the center of it all. My thoughts clear as I run. Sometimes the ruins of the stone ghosts block our path and we must circle around before we can continue. Occasionally, at crossings, I see the morning sun on our right as I glance down the long, narrow openings between the stone ghosts.

Neither of us say anything about Celeste, but she is never far from my thoughts. I am breathless when we reach the open place. The place of the trees.

Sierra's eyes go wide when she sees the trees spreading out before us in the midst of the stone ghosts. She rushes to touch one, running her hands along the thick bark. Soon she is wrapping her arms around the trunk of the tree and pressing her face up against it. Her eyes are full of light and she's smiling.

Something inside of me doesn't like this and I pull her away. The trees aren't what I want to share with her. What I want to show her is high above us and so I turn and point up and up to the stone ghost beside us that towers over all the others.

"There," I say, pointing to the top of the tower. "That's where we're going."

Just then we hear something, far off through the trees. It sounds like the pitter-patter of a gentle rain. But when I hold my hand up, there are no raindrops.

Pushing Sierra behind me, I back away as the pitter-patter gets closer and closer. Growls and yellow eyes in shadows precede the high-pitched howls that tell me what comes. "Wolves, the wolves that live within the shadows of the trees." I don't have to tell Sierra to run. She's running as fast as I've ever seen her run, faster even than yesterday.

The way to the front stairs of the tower is blocked, but I know there's another way. We scramble around and through the ruins with the howls so close it seems the wolves are at our heels.

I don't want to look back, but sometimes I do and catch glimpses of the wolves. Mostly they are indistinct, obscured by shadows, but sometimes they are clear and close. "Three at least, maybe more. Hurry!"

I push Sierra into an opening. Soon we are ascending stone stairs in dim light. The wolves have never before followed me up the stairs but I can hear them howling behind us.

Echoes make it hard to tell how close they are, so we climb and run, climb and run. We continue for as long as we can, until I'm certain the wolves have stopped coming after us. Even then though, they continue howling.

I settle into an easy pace because I know the climb will be a long one. Sierra looks uncertain, but I try to reassure her by squeezing her hand. "They've stopped. They'll go back to the trees."

The metal railing to our right is unreliable in places and missing in others. I keep Sierra away from it. Eventually, my legs tire and I see Sierra struggling to

71

keep up. We stop to rest in a place marked with the numbers: 4 and 9.

A missing section of the wall reveals how high we've climbed. Sierra is captivated by the view from these heights and she stares out at the ruins of the city as the wind whips at her long black hair. Stepping to her side, I point out the curious, green lady.

The green lady is far off in the distance, within the expanse. Though she's partially buried, she's a thing of beauty, with her head raised and her eyes staring up into the sky. In one hand, she holds a book—a book that I've always imagined is like the one Luke gave me for safekeeping. Her other hand is raised in the air and she's holding something but I don't know what it is. From this distance, the lady looks small but I know she isn't, as Luke and I went to her one day to try to learn her secrets.

"Ready to continue?" I say, pointing up the stairs. When Sierra steps away from the opening, her cheeks are red from the coolness of the air. I touch her face with the back of my hand and smile, remembering how Luke touched my cheek in just this way.

For a time, it's as if there are three of us climbing. I hear Luke's footsteps as his voice rings in my ears. He's telling me what we'll do when we reach the top and I think that he's playing with me because he does that sometimes. "When it comes, close your eyes and jump. Don't think about it, just jump. You're listening to me, aren't you? This is very important, because if you hesitate you'll miss it and then you'll jump into empty air."

He's not talking about the trucks in the wastes. He's talking about the trains that glide on air.

"Luke, I miss you," I say, my words a half-voiced whisper. "You wanted me to not be like the others and I'm trying. I am. Come back so I can show you. I've changed. I see. I feel or at least I want to believe I do. If you were here, you'd know and then I'd know..."

Sierra's eyes are on mine, I realize, but thankfully the wind has grown so loud and strong that my whispers are swallowed up. "Not much farther," I say loudly, pointing to the faded 7 and 6 on the wall.

Sierra is struggling with her steps and I am too but it's a good feeling, like when I'm running across the expanse with the trucks just ahead. If Luke were here, he'd be grinning and I'd be asking him why he's grinning and he'd say, "Because I'm here, in this special place, with you. Because we both know what's ahead and because we both know what we're about to do."

Sierra grabs my hand in both of hers and brings me back to the now. I realize I'm about to step into nothingness and pull back quickly. The wind is icy now and stronger, coming in gusts. I grip Sierra's hand in mine as we turn to survey our surroundings.

I can feel her shiver as she stands beside me. We've reached the top and the only thing separating us from the emptiness is the broken platform we've climbed up onto. Parts of walls remain in a few places, but mostly the space around us is open.

The platform is very thick so even though I pick my way around gaping holes in the floor beneath us, I am confident of my steps. Sierra is less certain, I can tell, and she follows mostly because of the grip of my hand in hers.

As I turn to look toward Central, I hear a familiar sound and know it is good that I spent so much time watching Luke skulk around here. I rush over to the only place where a section of wall can conceal us from what approaches. I kneel down and Sierra crouches beside me.

"What type of machine?" Sierra asks.

"An airtrain."

The train glides towards us on invisible rails, its lights flashing. As I toss Sierra my pack, I'm excited and it doesn't matter that the ground is so far below us. Without hesitation, I stand and take a few steps back. As I run and throw myself into the jump, I am a bird without wings, dangling in the air. When I land on top of one of the train cars, I remember to allow my momentum to carry me on and down to my knees. I look back at Sierra as I am whisked away, knowing my lips are parted in a wide grin.

The wind whips at me and it's difficult, but I stand and raise a hand in the air like the curious, green lady. Then I simply enjoy the ride, the rush of the air, as I sweep past the ruins of the broken city.

As I lean my head back and close my eyes, I feel the steady thrumming of the train. Sun and shadow alternately bathe my face. I begin to see things. A flutter of cloth. A whisper of raindrops. A tiny hand reaching up. Memories perhaps, though not mine.

It doesn't take long for the train to complete its circuit and before long I am racing back toward Sierra. "Catch me," I shout as I jump.

# Chapter 9

Node: 100

The airtrain whooshes away. Sierra is staring at me wide-eyed when I reach her and wrap my arms around her. "Your turn," I say, pushing her toward the opening.

"I don't want to," Sierra says, her voice trembling.

"Not alone, together," I say, taking her hand and lacing my fingers in between hers. "Jump when I tell you. Don't think about it."

The train makes its circuit quickly.

Readying myself, I take in a deep breath. Then I shout, "Jump!"

We jump together, Sierra a half step behind me. I land on my feet this time, Sierra doesn't. She goes down to her haunches but comes up quickly. She's a little shaken up, though no worse for the wear.

I feel uneasy. I've pushed her too hard. If Luke were here, he wouldn't have made her jump before she was ready. I know this, but I needed her to be ready. I did. I do.

"You okay?" I ask, shouting over the wind which seems to blow even harder as we start into a turn.

Sierra nods. "Is it always here?" Her voice seems a far off whisper, but I know she's shouting too or at least trying to shout.

Smiling, I sit down and pull Sierra with me. It will be easier to keep our balance if we're low to the ground.

Sierra inches toward me, her eyes regarding the ruins we're passing. I can tell she has many questions, but I don't know why the ruins are on one side of us and the trees are on the other side. I don't know why the airtrain makes a big circuit through the broken city and comes back each time to the same places. I don't know why it doesn't stop or slow or speed up. I don't know why it runs so high up in the air. I just know that it's here.

"I guess so," I finally say, "but I don't know for certain."

Sierra presses against me. "Does anyone?"

"Luke maybe," I say, shrugging. "He's the one who showed me. I don't know who showed him."

Wind rushes louder now as we race through another turn. High above, the sun shines down on us. Over my left shoulder, I catch glimpses of something glistening between the trees and without looking, I know it's the lake where we collect water when the rains stop.

Far off, in front of us, I see faintly the place where I know Central is, even though I can't see Central itself. I look for the watchers in the tower, but I can't see them either. I think of Celeste, but don't speak her name.

Sierra's uncomfortable. It shows in her eyes. "Lean your head back, close your eyes," I say.

Sierra looks at me quizzically.

"Like this," I say demonstrating.

Sierra leans her head back but doesn't close her eyes until I cover them with my hand. For a time, we simply enjoy the ride. Listening, but not seeing as sun and shadow flicker by.

As we start into another turn, I know we've missed the platform and our chance to disembark. Sierra seems to realize this too as she turns to look back. "It's okay," I say, "nothing to worry about."

Sierra frowns. She doesn't say anything but she presses more tightly against me.

We make two more circuits before we start back. Jumping from the train to the platform is a challenge, but I coax Sierra through it.

The return trek is uneventful. Thankfully, there are no wolves waiting when we reach the landing on the ground floor, no shadows to haunt our footsteps as we walk to Central. All in all, the day is a welcome distraction from what would have been a day fretting over something we had no control over.

When I close my eyes to sleep, I see it. Wind in trees. Rain on grass. Sunshine through clouds. I am sand. Sand cast at the heavens. I am nothing.

# Chapter 10

Node: 010

Days pass before Celeste starts to become one of us and I am less worried for her. It is Sierra's patience and steadfast attention that nurtures this change as much as anything else. A profound change has found Sierra as well. Her voice has bloomed, just as my words and thoughts have.

Everything is so different. I'm certain I know now what my heart knows. What Luke wanted me to know all along. I feel. I know. I remember. I remember what is and what was.

Breakfast is a meager affair with most of us sitting at long tables off the main hall. It's where I find Sierra and Celeste when I awake.

"Good morning," I tell Sierra as I sit and brush back Celeste's hair. "How is she today?"

"Better, stronger," Sierra says. "She listens and I know she wants to be like us. I know. Isn't that right, Celeste?"

Celeste looks from Sierra to me. "It is."

Hearing her speak, I sweep my arms around her. "Already?" I ask, turning to Sierra.

"Already," Sierra confirms. "She started the day before yesterday. Guess what she said first?"

Sierra's first words had been "book" and "Cedes," in that order. Celeste always seemed more interested in the things in the book than in the book itself. "Plane? Truck? Train?"

"Truck. How did you know?"

I smile but don't answer. Few words pass between us while we quietly slurp up a thin pasty gruel. My thoughts turn inward. Each day brings me closer to my inevitable choice. I look out and see what should be there but isn't. I look out and see what is there and what is missing.

Matthew seems to sense the change. He sends me to gather or to stand watch but never to go out and look. He tries to keep Sierra and I apart, but I do my best to pass on what I know, what I've learned, what I've guessed, regardless.

Someone must take my place when I do the inevitable. When I leave Central and search for Luke. Luke has the answers I need. He knows much more than the truth of us. I know he does. The unspoken answers were always in his eyes, but I was never in a place where I could ask the questions that needed to be asked.

In contrast, I hold nothing back from Sierra. I answer the questions she doesn't yet know to ask. If those in Central are my family, like the families in the book, Sierra is my sister. My true sister. My real sister. A sister not just of my blood but of my heart.

Removing the book from my pack, I give it to Sierra and say, "Take this with you today."

Matthew is at the head of the table. Linc, Chevy, Austin and Dakota are seated nearby. When Matthew sees the book, he pushes his bowl away and jumps up. Walking towards us, he shouts, "This is wrong. What you're doing is wrong."

I stand and turn to him. This confrontation has been a long time coming. I don't mean to show my anger, but perhaps my eyes betray me as much as my words do. "What? What? Haven't you enough regulars to do whatever you tell them? Do you really need more?"

Matthew sticks an accusatory finger in my face. "This is about right and wrong. Nothing else. You've no right. What you're doing is wrong, against the lore, the laws."

The whole of Central is gathering around our growing spectacle. I don't care. My thoughts have been building to this moment for days. "Which lore, which laws?" I say quickly and without thinking. "What is wrong with learning, knowing what is and what was?"

Matthew brushes back long black hair from his steel gray eyes. His icy expression is a dangerous warning. "Do you want me to order you to relinquish the book? Is that what it will take to ensure I never see it again?"

I'm small but I stand up to him. "Luke would never—"

Matthew's hypnotic eyes probe my depths. He clenches and unclenches his right hand, almost as if he wants to strike me down. "Do you see Luke anywhere about? I don't. Luke has forsaken us."

I lean forward, returning his stare and ignoring Sierra's hand against my arm. She's squeezing as tightly as she can, as if that will silence me. "Luke would never leave willingly. Never."

"Are you implying something? Are you calling me a *liar?*"

I know to proceed carefully. "I've said no such thing. I merely suggest that Luke may not be able to return to us. He may be in trouble, lost or injured. If you let us go out and search again, we may yet find him."

Snatching the book from the table, Matthew turns to throw it into the fire, but just as suddenly, he pulls back, raising the book into the air and turning to look at those who have gathered around. "Should this burn?"

Instead of waiting for an answer, he hurls the book. Jumping up, I block his throw and catch the book in my chest. I'm angry, as I fall backward and my butt slams against the ground. As Matthew stands over me, I shout up at him, "If Luke were here, you'd never try such a thing. Luke should have been the one in charge all along. Not you."

Matthew glares at me but says nothing else. When he stalks away, Sierra and Celeste help me back to the table.

"You okay?" Sierra whispers.

I nod, make sure no one sees my tears as I secure the book in my pack. "I wish you could have known Luke as I knew him."

Sierra says, "I knew Luke. I know. What happened."

"What happened to us was the machines." My words are bitter; my thoughts, distant.

Sierra squeezes my hand and there's an urgency, intensity, in her deep green eyes. "Not us, Luke."

Her words pull me back to the here and now. "Luke? What do you mean? What do you know?"

"I know what happened. It's what I've wanted to tell you, but I couldn't find the words." Sierra pauses while my eyes urge her to continue. She looks to Celeste, her voice dropping to a whisper. "I was with Luke."

"With Luke when?"

"When he left us. When he walked into the expanse." I could hear the truth in her voice. "He told me you would protect me and that I would show you the way."

"How would you show me the way?"

"He didn't say. He told me to stay close to you, to learn what I needed to learn. He told me not to be sad."

I can't believe what I'm hearing. I want to scream, "You knew? You knew?" But I don't. My thoughts turn inward. We sit for a time saying nothing. I think about Luke, about why he left us, about what his words mean.

I watch Celeste too. She will be like us. I've made sure. Already she is starting to see what others don't.

Sometimes I watch as Sierra tries to teach Celeste from the book. Sierra doesn't know I watch but I do, for it is the only way to be certain our work continues, that hope continues—and hope now is something I truly understand. Just as I now understand what it is to dream. However did I live without dreams? How bleak my life must have been.

And yet, it wasn't long ago that I was like Matthew's regulars. At times, I wonder what Luke saw in me that made him know I was the one. The one to follow his path. Or was it that he took a chance on me? A chance that he, perhaps, didn't give others.

These are, of course, some few of the many questions I should have asked but hadn't. Some few of the questions that only Luke can answer.

Absently, I listen while Matthew speaks our lore. He looks straight at me when he speaks the Fourth Law and I see the plans turn in his mind. Then, he assigns instructions. "Diggers: James, Mark. Gatherers: Dakota, Austin, Chevy, Cedes," he says. "Watchers: Linc, Jetta, Rabbit. Beyonders: Celeste, Sierra. Trekkers…"

After Celeste and Sierra's names are called, I stop listening. I know Matthew's eyes are on me when I walk away.

My thoughts are spinning. It's the first time Matthew has put Celeste and Sierra together. The first time he's

asked them to go out and look. It seems a punishment—
a punishment for me.

Wasting no time, I put the book in my pack and step
to Dakota, Austin, and Chevy. I lead them down the dark
hall and we climb the stone stairs together.

After unbarring the steel doors and letting in the
bright light, I wait and listen, my heart thumping in my
chest. The silence that greets me is reassuring and soon I
step out cautiously into the sunlight. "I'm Cedes," I say
to the sun.

"Come," Sierra says to the others as she waves them
through the doors. She guides Linc, Jetta and Rabbit to
the tower. "Go, watch," she says, making circles of her
thumb and fingers and put them in front of her eyes.
Before Sierra and Celeste begin the long walk to the
empty places, I wave them over.

"Thank you for before, but I was wrong. I shouldn't
have disrespected Matthew in front of the others. I
should've waited until later and talked to him privately."

Sierra puts her hand on my elbow. "No, you had
every right. Matthew started it. If he didn't want to be
challenged in front of the others, he should've waited."

Celeste takes my other hand. I see understanding, sympathy, in her eyes.

As I shoulder my pack and I watch them go, I realize Sierra has taken my place in the order of things. Somehow, I know it should bother me, but it doesn't. Instead, I find it liberating, as if a burden has been lifted and I know with certainty the time for me to leave Central has come. I give Dakota, Austin, and Chevy their packs and wave them away, saying, "Go, gather. Find what you can and return."

Instead of going with them like I'm supposed to, I turn away and start walking in the opposite direction. Slowly, I walk past the stone ghosts. Eventually, I come to the empty places and begin the long climb up the hill. At times, I catch glimpses of Sierra and Celeste ahead of me. I hear Sierra talking to Celeste as I once talked to her, but I make sure they don't see or hear me even when they turn to look back to the safety of Central before hesitantly continuing on.

# Chapter 11

Node: 011

Throughout the morning and into the day, I watch Sierra and Celeste from a shadowed recess at the top of the stairs. I know I could join them but I want to wait and watch, to make sure they're ready, to make sure they no longer need me.

It's strange to hear Celeste speak. Her voice is beautiful, melodic, a lot like Sierra's but with more depth. Her progress is surprising, a feat made even greater as I've kept the book mainly for my own. I know this is selfish. I will tell Sierra the book is hers to keep before I go.

My growth has led me to new questions about who and what we are. I wonder too about the machines, about what we are to them, about what want they have of us.

Matthew is wrong to say we are nothing to the machines, to say the machines have no need of us. They certainly have some want of us. But what kind of want? Why do they cage us? Are they afraid of us? Do they study us as I study Sierra and Celeste?

My foot slips as I shift in my hiding space. Celeste turns and stares straight into the shadows—straight at me. I stop breathing and keep still waiting for her to look away, but her stare lingers. There are questions in her eyes and fear.

Fear of me, perhaps. Fear of the unknown, certainly. I want to say, "It's just me, Cedes." But I don't. Instead, I hold still and focus on quieting my breaths.

It's Sierra who draws her attention away, gripping her shoulder and pointing to the distance. Even without the field glasses she's using to stare into the far corner of the wastes, I know what she sees. It's the beginnings of a convoy.

As it's the first convoy of the day, I relax, knowing there won't be any white trucks. White trucks are only in the second convey of the day, if at all. Because otherwise, all the trucks are gray. Except once. That time there had been black trucks too.

When Sierra and Celeste start running down the ridge, I'm certain something is wrong. But my field glasses tell me otherwise as I start counting and find the white trucks exactly where they should be even if this isn't the second convoy of the day.

After removing the book from my pack and putting it carefully on a rock in the recess, I start running down the ridge too. Sierra and Celeste are out in the expanse well ahead of me. The roar of the driverless trucks masks the sound of my feet.

The distance between us begins to close as Celeste tires. Soon I am just behind them running up the hill as the convoy races through the cutaway.

Sierra's wide smile says everything and without looking back, she says, "I knew you would be here when it was time. I knew it."

"Faster," I shout. "Almost to the jump. Don't hesitate. Just jump," I say. My words are more for Celeste than Sierra, though both nod their heads in understanding.

"That one," Sierra says, pointing to the second to last white truck.

"Is she ready for this? Ready to know?" I ask.

"She is," Sierra replies.

As I work my way between them, I grab both their hands, adjusting my pace and path to reach the truck before it cuts its way through the hill and is gone. I steal a glance at Celeste just to see the look of wonder and excitement on her face.

Never having jumped with three before, I'm excited too. At the top of the hill, I rush our pace to correct our timing before I shout, "Jump. Jump now!"

# Chapter 12

Node: 100

With nothing beneath our feet after we jump, it's as if we're running on air. Celeste cries out, "Wow!" An instant later, we're landing on the back of a truck and dropping down flat against the canvas. I roll over onto my back and lay there, trying to catch my breath as the wind whips at us.

There's a problem though. We've landed on the first gray truck in the end sequence and not on the last white truck.

Wind whips at me as I stand and try to think about what we should do. I've no idea what's in the gray trucks.

Matthew seemed to know and he was terribly afraid of even the thought of ending up on one of the gray trucks.

Laughter drops from Sierra's eyes when she sees what I see. She looks back, ahead, and points. "Run," she shouts. Taking Celeste's hand in hers, she begins running up the truck.

The cab of the truck is the same height as the back, but she doesn't stop there. She jumps across to the white truck ahead. I follow, my heart in my throat as I jump from one truck to the other.

Before I even land Sierra scrambles to the edge. "Hold on here," she tells Celeste, demonstrating. "Drop down and then swing in."

She goes over without hesitation and hangs there, holding on with both hands. Celeste and I follow and then we all swing our way into the back of the white truck.

Soon we are making our way forward past tie-downs to the first of three containers. The large metal box has solid sides, but I know from experience the front is barred and can be opened. Since there are three of us, I wonder for a moment if we could take two with us. What would

Matthew say if we did? How would he explain this "miracle" to the others? Would he say two of us fell from the sky? Or would he invent a new mistruth to explain away the anomaly?

It's a lot to think about in the span of a few moments. A few breaths. But the questions come whether I want them to or not. I wonder too if perhaps we are all anomalies to the machines. Some strange error that they write off, as we write them off.

We exist here. They exist there. Separate. Different. But perhaps in some ways the same, for they want us just as we want us. What they want us for, I don't know. What we want us for, I couldn't say. More of us isn't any better than less of us, except that somehow it is better. Perhaps, better only in some small way I don't know or understand, but better all the same. Perhaps, the machines don't know or understand exactly why they want us either.

I pull back the canvas curtain and reveal the container's contents. The human inside is chained by his hands and feet, standing upright. He is thin and tall, as tall and thin as Luke, but perhaps not as tall as Matthew. His face is partially obscured by thick tangles of wires, connectors and tubes, but his brown eyes are clear and open.

Celeste doesn't like what she sees. "Why?" she asks.

Sierra tells Celeste what I told her. "This is the truth of us. Don't look away. You have to see and remember. You have to remember what was and know why we must never tell the others."

"It's time," I tell myself, knowing that taking two isn't the answer. The answers are out there beyond the wastes. They are with Luke, if I can find Luke.

As I turn to Sierra, I'm certain she knows what I'm thinking. She reaches out and embraces me even before I can reach out to her. "Sisters," I whisper to her. "We'll always be sisters, even if we're apart."

Celeste's eyes show she doesn't fully understand what's happening. I know she wants to because that's reflected in her eyes too and because she wraps her arms around us both.

"Sisters always," Sierra says back.

"Sisters," Celeste says. "Sisters always."

"The book is yours," I tell Sierra. "Look for a recess on the far side of the ridge. You'll find the book inside."

She smiles against her sudden sadness. "I knew at breakfast, even before you knew. I'm going to miss you. It won't be the same without you. You must promise, promise to return someday, when you can, no matter what."

A sudden rumbling within the truck reminds me we've been onboard much too long. I don't know if I can or should promise such a thing, but I say, "I promise. I promise. If I can, I will."

"Not if," Sierra says. "Make a promise, keep it, as I promise to continue without you, to do the best I can without you."

"A promise." We all know time is running out. There's no need to say anything more. "I'll cut while you free our new brother. I trust you've selected a name?"

Sierra nods. "I have."

As I start cutting, I shout back, "Quickly now, before it's too late."

Our new brother is Dasher. I learn that much before Celeste and Sierra drop away with him and are gone from sight. The wait that follows is the hard part, for once they're gone I decide to not just to stay and see what's beyond the expanse. I decide to stay and take Dasher's place in the container.

I do this because I know the answers are out there, but I no longer think Luke has them. I think the machines have them—and I'm going to get them.

Celeste's black jumpsuit is in my backpack. I put it on before I discard my pack and old clothes, then I step into the metal box. Attaching the wires is easier than I thought it would be. The connectors attach easily and I've removed them so many times I know where each goes. The hard part is forcing the tubes down my throat before I attach the large, square connector to the back of my skull.

Pain fills me. Everything becomes still. Everything careens to darkness. And then I am no more.

The story continues with:

# After the Machines
# Episode Two: Transition

## This Mortal Coil

# About the Author

Robert Stanek is author of the #1 bestselling ELVES OF THE REACHES, an epic fantasy series, currently comprising eight books, which has been translated into twelve languages; the #1 bestselling MAGIC LANDS, a young adult series comprising two books and counting, which has been translated into seven languages; and the #1 bestselling POCKET CONSULTANTS, a computer technology series comprising 35 books and counting, which have been translated into 21 languages.

Robert is also author of the #1 bestselling BUGVILLE CRITTERS, a children's series comprising 28 books and counting; #1 bestselling BUGVILLE LEARNING, an educational series comprising 31 books and counting; the #1 bestselling BUGVILLE JR, a children's series comprising 26 books and counting; and the #1 bestselling THE PIECES OF THE PUZZLE, a mystery thriller novel for adults.

In his fiction writing, Robert transports readers to many imagined worlds. Robert's early fiction work has many influences, including JRR Tolkien, C S Lewis, Anne McCaffrey, H G Wells, and Ray Bradbury.

In his long, distinguished writing career, Robert's books have been distributed and/or published by Simon & Schuster, Random House, Macmillan, Pearson, Microsoft, O'Reilly, and others. In 2007, Robert founded Go Indie, an organization dedicated to supporting independent publishers, authors, and booksellers, and over the past few years Go Indie has helped hundreds of independents.

Dubbed 'A Face Behind the Future' in the 1990's by *The Olympian*, Robert's been helping to shape the future of the written word for over two decades. Robert's 150th book was published in 2013.

## Select Acclaim for Robert Stanek...

"Robert Stanek is one of our most featured and respected Kids & Young Adults, K-12 Educators and Kids authors."

--The Audio Book Store

"Stanek [has] a penchant for clear and simple prose. He also prefers swift, action-oriented scenes. Solidly built. Stanek moves among his main characters with ease, always switching at a climactic moment to maintain suspense. The accessible, brisk language keeps things moving."

--Foreword Magazine

"Sure to attract fans of graphic novels and classic Tolkien alike. Stanek will likely draw a cult following. This guarantees fans, and those fans will be ready to wield their swords against the Dark Lord in Stanek's next installment."

-- VOYA, the leading magazine for YA librarians

"Word of mouth turned it into a bestseller. Very satisfying."

-- The Fantasy Guide

**Select Achievements for Robert Stanek and his Ruin Mist books...**

#1 Fiction, Audible (12 weeks, 2005)

Top 50 Sci-fi/Fantasy, Amazon (26 weeks, 2002)

Top 10 Fiction, Audible (25 weeks, 2005)

Top 50 Fiction, Audible (52 weeks, 2005-2006)

Top 10 Kids & YA, Audible (180 weeks, 2005-2007)

#1 Featured Book Audible June-July 2005

Featured in Cover Story, Publisher's Weekly (2009)

Featured in VOYA (2007)

Featured in Complete Idiots Guide to Elves and Fairies (2005)

Featured in Ancient Art of Faery Magick (2005)

Popular Series Fiction for Middle School and Teen Readers (2005, 2008)

Top 10 Recommended Author -- SciFi Bookcase (2004 - 2012)

Top 10 Book -- SciFi Bookcase (2004 - 2012)

Top 20 Author -- RateItAll (2005 - 2012)

A Top 100 Fantasy -- The Fantasy 100 (2005 - 2007)

**Robert Stanek and his books have also been featured in...**

The Olympian, The Journal of Electronic Defense, The Publisher's Weekly Cover Story, The Parenting Magazine, VOYA, BookWire, Children's Writer, Children's Bookshelf, Library Journal, School Library Journal, The News Tribune, and more.

## Also by Robert Stanek

**Kingdoms and the Elves of the Reaches #1, 2, 3, 4:**
Winds of Change
Seeds of Dissent
Pawn of Dragons
Tower of Destiny

**In the Service of Dragons #1, 2, 3, 4:**
A Clash of Heroes
A Dance of Swords
A Storm of Shields
A Reign of Dragons

**Guardians of the Dragon Realms #1, 2:**
The Dragon, the Wizard & the Great Door
A Legacy of Dragons

**Dragons of the Hundred Worlds #1, 2:**
Breath of Fire
Living Fire

**A Daughter of Kings #1, 2, 3, 4:**
Betrayal
Deliverance
Rebirth
Discord

**The Pieces of the Puzzle #1, 2:**
The Pieces of the Puzzle
The Cards in the Deck

**Thank you for buying this book!**

Find out about special offers, free book giveaways, amazing deals, and exclusive content! Plus get updates and more when you join Robert Stanek on Facebook at https://www.facebook.com/Robert.Stanek.Author. Visit us online at http://www.reagentpress.com/current.html.